Amadou's Zoo

Rebecca Walsh

PAGE
STREET
KIDS

This is Amadou, and this is his teacher Madame Minier. Amadou's class is going to the zoo. It is an old, old zoo. Madame Minier says it was built for a king. But Amadou doesn't hear that.

Sometimes . . .

Amadou's imagination wanders.

And right now . . .

all he can do is dream about the animals at the zoo!

But first, Amadou and his class have to wait a *long, long, long* time for the train. In a line.

"Please wait patiently with the group," Madame Minier says.

Madame Minier loves being organized. But Amadou's daydreams
don't like staying in line any more than he does!

When they *finally* arrive at the zoo, Madame Minier says,
"Stay focused, and please listen carefully."

Amadou *is* listening . . .
to the sound of flamingos calling and dancing together.

"Amadou! Both feet on the ground please. Let us make our way quietly to see the lion."

Amadou wonders how lions can be quiet when they can . . .

ROAR!

"Amadou! Shhhhh, and please don't wander," Madame Minier says.

But Amadou's mind has already wandered.

There is so much to explore!

"Class, did you know that elephants can't actually run?" Madame Minier asks. "They always have one foot on the ground."

Madame Minier loves the signs; they are full of *facts*.

But Amadou imagines the elephants
must feel like they're running anyway.

"Class," says Madame Minier, "please pick a tank and read the entire description before moving on. We cannot learn unless we slow down and pay attention."

Amadou's attention is on the tiny, wise eyes of the tortoise who moves so slowly and has known so many years. His classmates follow along.

"Class, we are nearing the end of our trip," says Madame Minier.

"Please take a moment to collect your belongings—"

"Class! Where are you going?"

"Here we are!" says Amadou.

"Let me help you

see the zoo

the way we do!"

Amadou loves to explore. Madame Minier loves that too.

And today, Amadou has shown her that sometimes the best way to explore is through imagination.

This is Amadou, these are his classmates, and this is his teacher Madame Minier. They have been at the zoo *all day* and this is what they've seen:

Animals who dance, roar, prowl, run, wander, flutter, climb, play, explore, learn,

and maybe even use *their* imaginations.

For Naomi and Max.
And for the real Amadou, wherever you are.

Copyright © 2020 Rebecca Walsh

First published in 2020 by Page Street Kids,
an imprint of
Page Street Publishing Co.
27 Congress Street, Suite 105
Salem, MA 01970
www.pagestreetpublishing.com

Distributed by Macmillan, sales in Canada by The Canadian Manda Group

20 21 22 23 24 CCO 5 4 3 2 1

ISBN-13: 978-1-62414-884-2
ISBN-10: 1-62414-884-0

CIP data for this book is available from the Library of Congress.

This book was typeset in ITC Century Std Book.
The illustrations were done in watercolor and acrylic gel medium.

Printed and bound in Shenzhen, Guangdong, China

Page Street Publishing uses only materials from suppliers who are committed to
responsible and sustainable forest management.

Page Street Publishing protects our planet by donating to nonprofits like The Trustees,
which focuses on local land conservation.